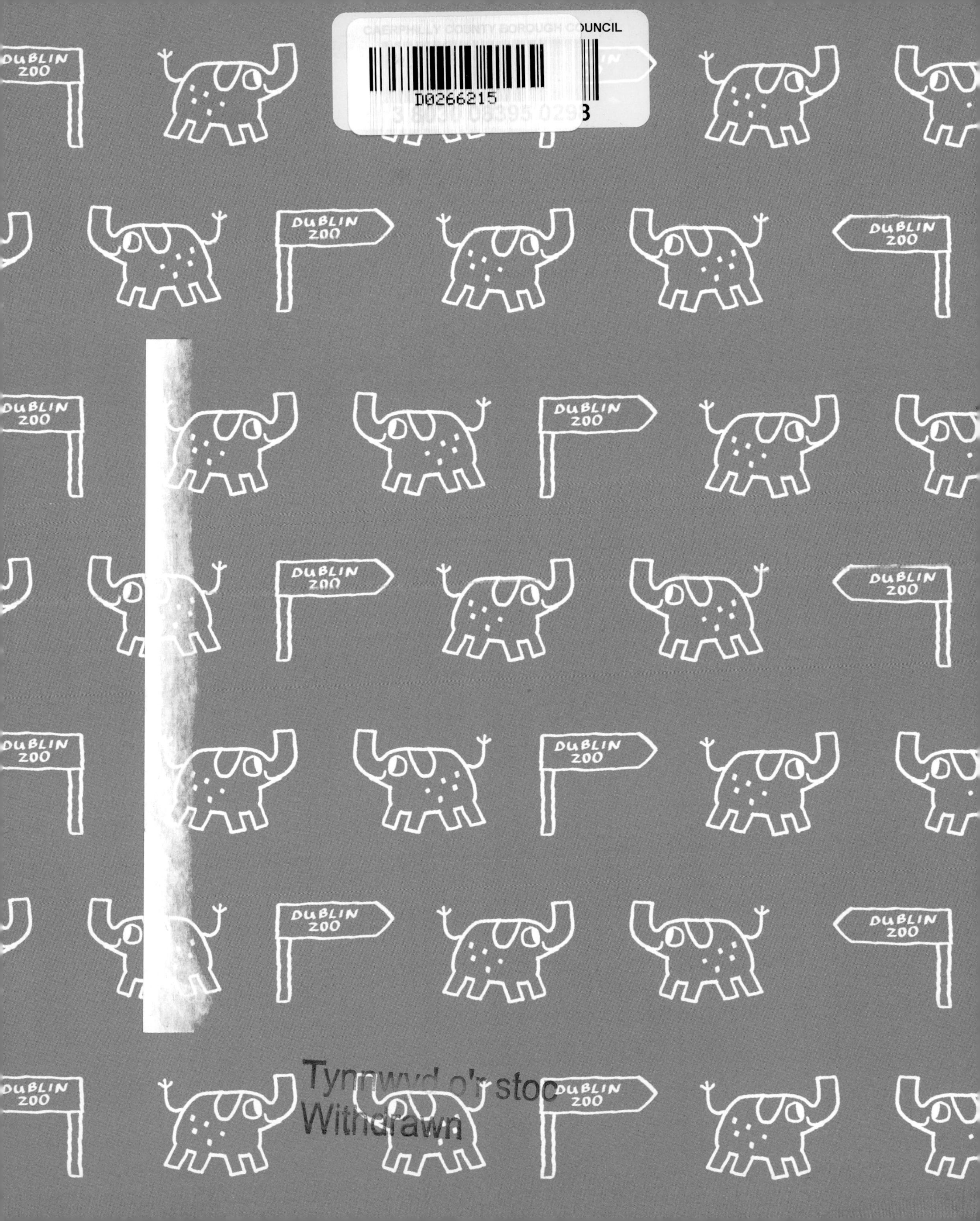

CAERPHILLY COUNTY BOROUGH COUNCIL
D0266215
Tynnwyd o'r stoc
Withdrawn

THE O'BRIEN PRESS
DUBLIN

House where Kitty and her big sister Clara live
Áras an Uachtaráin
The Phoenix Park
DUBLIN ZOO
Farmleigh
COO!
The Spire
River Liffey
The Ha'penny Bridge
Guinness storehouse
St. Patrick's cathedral
well?

My big sister is always bored.

The only time she's **not** bored is when she's doing...

It's the summer holidays and yep, you guessed it...

...my sister's really...

So Dad says:

I'm going to **draw pictures** of all the animals so I can show them to Mam when she gets home from work.

My sister only wants to see the **red pandas**. Other than that, the zoo is...

I head straight for the **fruit bats**.
They're sleeping because it's daytime, so they're good ones to start with.
You're so weird.
Here's me - drawing like **crazy**.
draw
draw
draw

And here's my fruit bat drawing

This is the right way, so don't turn the page around!
These are the WINGS
Bats are the only mammals that can FLY!
QUESTION
Do bats in Australia sleep standing-up?
ANSWER
Hmmmm, maybe.
G'day!
When they sleep they use their wings like a BLANKET!

Next I draw the **elephants**.

They're having a bath, so this one is a bit trickier.

Dad says: 'A little bit of water never hurt anyone.'

'Yeah!' I say and my sister gives me a **dirty look**.

Here's my **elephant** drawing

Over to the **giraffes**. My sister is still wet from the elephants.

The zookeeper is bringing them some food. It must be lunchtime.

They look hungry.

My giraffe drawing
I ran out of room for the HEAD, but you get the idea!
Giraffes are the tallest animals on the planet.
Even a BABY is taller than a human!
da da!
Me "resting" my tongue!
Giraffes rest their tongue by hanging it out the side of their MOUTH!

My sister finds the **red pandas,** and starts to take about a million **selfies**.

At first the red panda looks a bit surprised.

But then he just ignores my sister, who's being a **total pain**.

Here's just ONE of my sister's photos!
And here's my drawing!
Red Pandas are NOT related to Black & White pandas!
Huh?
They have FUR on the soles of their feet so they don't SLIP in the snow!
This one WAVED at me...honestly!

Now over to the **tapirs**.

My sister likes these too and she even says my drawing '*isn't terrible*'.

I say she can have some paper if she wants to draw too, but she says '**Nah**'.

The baby tapir is having a nap. He's got stripes for camouflage. His mam is getting some food.

Here's my tapir drawing

Tapirs have LONG NOSES
which they use to
GRAB FOOD
They are
nothing
to do with
ELEPHANTS!
Tapirs are
brilliant
swimmers and use
their NOSES like
SNORKELS!
They come from
the BRAZILIAN
rain forest

'Why don't you like
drawing anymore?'
I ask my sister.

'Drawing's for *babies.*'

'You're quite good
at it though,'
she says.

This **tiger** is really
enjoying the
sunshine.

Here's my tiger drawing

Next we visit the **sea lions**.

The zookeeper has trained them so she can keep an eye on their health.

They let her check their eyes, ears, noses and flippers...

...and she rewards them with fish!

My sea lion drawing

These **monkeys** are called **macaques**.

They're all grooming each other, which is their favourite thing to do.

'Do you remember that time you showed me how to draw cat faces?' I ask my sister.

'And then we used to have cat-face-drawing competitions all the time?'

'Yeah,' she says. 'But that was ages ago.'

My macaque drawing

We go over to the **rhinos** where there's a new baby.

Both me and my sister think he is the **cutest** thing we've ever seen.

He's running around and around...

...and keeps bumping into things because he's a bit blind.

Here's my baby rhino drawing
(my sister did the hearts)
Rhinos (even the BIG ones)
are really fast runners!
whoOOsh!
They have
VERY BAD
EYESIGHT
There's
no need to
shout!
...and brilliant
HEARING
excuse
me...

Last stop the **meerkats**.

It's their dinner-time.

'You're still really good at drawing,' I say to my sister.

'Nah,' she says. '*Really*?'

Here's the meerkats
by me AND my sister!
Meerkats
have
DARK
CIRCLES
around their
eyes to help
with the
sun...
...a bit like
SUNGLASSES!
They stand up
straight when they
are looking out
for
DANGER...
...like a
security
guard!
They can eat
snakes and scorpions
without getting
poisoned!

draw draw draw
Hi girls, do you mind if I have a look?
ZOO
These are great!
Well, it's really all my sister. She's the artist.
Most people just take photos and they all look the same.
ZOO

Dad says we can, and Mam is going to come too.

V

Here's me with all my drawings.
Loads of people came...

...and I got my picture taken
with the zookeeper.

ZOO

Her name is
Susan.

Flash!

And of course my sister took a photo too.

Here it is...

First published 2018 by The O'Brien Press Ltd,
12 Terenure Road East, Rathgar, Dublin 6, Ireland.
D06 HD27
Tel: +353 1 4923333; Fax: +353 1 4922777
E-mail: books@obrien.ie
Website: www.obrien.ie
The O'Brien Press is a member of Publishing Ireland.

Copyright for text and illustrations © Sarah Bowie, 2018
Copyright for layout, editing and design
© The O'Brien Press Ltd

ISBN: 978-1-84717-949-4

All rights reserved. No part of this book may be reproduced or utilised in any way or by any means, electronic or mechanical, including photocopying, recording or by any information storage and retrieval system without permission in writing from the publisher.

10 9 8 7 6 5 4 3 2 1
23 22 21 20 19 18

Printed and bound in Poland by Białostockie Zakłady Graficzne S.A.
The paper in this book is produced using pulp from managed forests.

Published in: